ROBINSON IN CHRONOSTASIS

A SURREALIST
PSYCHOGEOGRAPHICAL
NON-ROMANCE

SAM JENKS
WITH KOJI TSUKADA
AND DAN JACKSON

SAM JENKS

Sam is a writer, queering psychogeography, strayed from the path, hopelessly lost. He uses fiction-auto-fiction-non-fiction-mash-up to approach his interest in landscapes and strangers in strange places. His short stories have been published in Fruit Journal, Queerlings and Litro. He is also Artistic Director of Out on the Page which supports LGBTQ+ writers worldwide.

KOJI TSUKADA

Koji is a post- contemporary artist and small antique-shop dealer living and working in Nagano,Japan. Between 2015 and 2018 he studied and practised art in Bath, UK. His particular interest in landscape, memory and myth led to studio installations that won the Porthleven Prize in 2017 and NG Art Creative Residency Prize in 2018. In the process he made a 3D photocopy/facsimile of a folding-pocket Kodak camera from 1904 which he'd bought in a Bath flea-market. This facsimile camera was used in the production of some of these photos.

DAN JACKSON

Dan is a London based designer with an avidity for literature, poetry and stories. His practice centres around using design and illustration to accompany, embellish and evoke the written word in publications and book covers. - *dan-jackson.com*

STEVE BENSON

Steve Benson, gay man, he/him;psychogeography, lgbt studies/Queer Theory, desuetudinousness, using hybrid genres and weave of text and image.
- *towardsutopia.wordpress.com*

"MEMORIES THAT HAVE SOMEHOW BROKEN LOOSE FROM ME".

This startlingly beautiful collaboration between Japanese photographer, Koji Tsukada, and writer Sam Jenks-and more latterly- book designer Dan Jackson, wears its lineage lightly. In fact, its past- via intratext and citation- is an intrinsic part of its present; and the weave is seamless.

This meditation of photographic captures - with counter-pointing and rhizomatic text -speaks of memory and time. How we inhabit the present; yet, simultaneously, the past(ours and others) via this very process of memory. How we try to armour ourselves against the oblivion of death by collecting, archiving, and recording; memorializing.

The reader is taken on a poignant meta-textual and visual adventure, a derive- along a highway and through a demesne; peopled by the friendly spectres of W G Sebald, Patrick Keiller, and Walter Benjamin, to name but three.

As well as being a (musical) fugue through vertical time and memory, it has the (studied) air of a Sebaldian fugue (in its sense of a dissociative psychological state, redolent of the scenes of disorientation and lostness of the narrator on Dunwich Heath in "Rings of Saturn"). Thus, at one, intense point- vividly conveyed in Jenks' signature (semi) epigrammatic language-Robinson recounts how he once stood in a council high-rise flat, frozen in angoisse, vertigo, and confusion. Indeed, Sebald is overtly yet unobtrusively threaded throughout this narrative.

The dual narrator/collaborator format of Keiller's Robinson films is there too; with there being a silent PRESENCE (in a similar way to the ghosted narratorial voice in the Keiller films), with the shadowy companion (here the photographer, who often portrays shades, ghosts, in the form of found objects, and, thus, memories).

Walter Benjamin is also evoked in the constellations (LPS, books, espresso cups) the narrator collects in his prose; which Tsukada images in his (loosely) corresponding captures; remnants of capitalist, superceded enterprises.

Another presence, adding a further layer to the (multi-) texture, is the book's designer, Dan Jackson. Dan adds shadings (hommage to Sebald's old postcards- complete with grainy ambiguity -interpellated into his prose-fiction, perhaps); he weaves in skew, vertical and horizontal lines, to mirror the various ways in which we experience time and memory. He also incorporates cryptic square boxes, which have a spectral miniaturisation effect, as another, parallel melody to the main composition, as if we are seeing the material down a vertiginous well of time. This makes the tripartite collaboration-through time, space, and memory-poignantly complete.

Whether you are aware of these inter/intra-texts, or not, is by no means the only point at stake (though they certainly FURTHER enrich a sparse yet strangely fruity stasis of time): indeed, Jenks and Tsukada and Jackson have created a (self-) standing-stone to (attempt to...) outlast time itself. This book is a fluid monument; a small tome. You should grasp it for dear life.

Steven Benson, 8.12.21.

ROBINSON IN CHRONOSTASIS

All the books that I've kept over the years are shelved on the wall behind my desk. A poster of a farmhand from a Paul Strand exhibition, an impressionist portrait in oils by Paskalis Anastasi, and a postcard of Joe Orton, hang around the other walls like memories that have somehow broken loose from me.

////////

<

ROBINSON IN CHRONOSTASIS

Before leaving to meet Koji at Society Café, I stood gazing out of my window at King Apple, the aged tree that stands in my garden, daydreaming that he might hold within his rings a record of the memories and longings of those who gazed into his branches.

ROBINSON IN CHRONOSTASIS

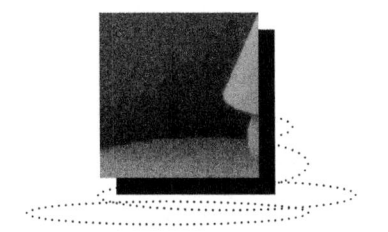

When I returned, I sat at my desk and took out my PACSA notebook with the Valencian-orange soft cover and reached for my pen, a Mitsubishi UB-157.

ROBINSON IN CHRONOSTASIS

I thought about the watch and the typewriter, they must have been about as old as King Apple; made for marking time and recording events, but with no actual or historical memory of their own; just archaeological wear and tear. What use does he have for them? Most days, he would rush in to the library, perch on the edge of a swivel chair for just a few minutes and connect with one of the Macs.

ROBINSON IN CHRONOSTASIS

My mind settled on one turbulent year in my life in which I moved home nine times. I wrote about a moment where, standing in a 19th floor council flat in Shepherds Bush, London, I felt confused and anxious, unsure if I was packing or unpacking the boxes and bags standing in front of me.

ROBINSON IN CHRONOSTASIS

////////

I never saw his living or studio spaces in Bath. I thought he might have lived amongst these shadows until I saw the warehouse trolley in the left of the picture and realised that he too was packing or unpacking in another space, perhaps another time.

ROBINSON IN CHRONOSTASIS

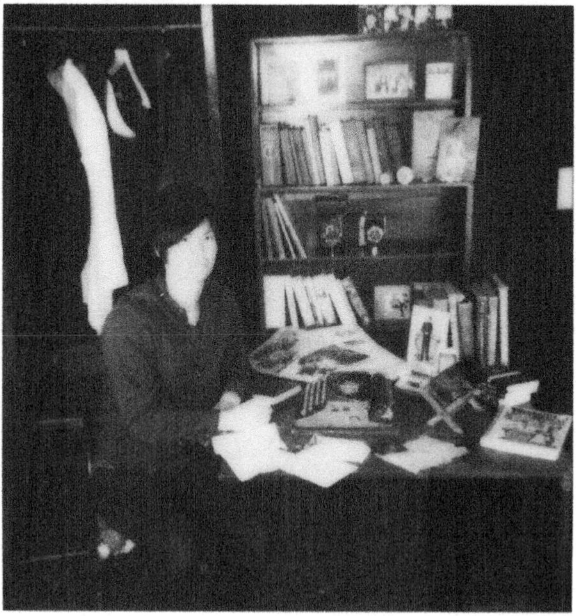

I imagine the contents of my own self-portrait. Wearing the tan corduroy shirt by Nicole Farhi, I'd be holding the aluminium-capped Faber-Castell pencil pressed against a well worn notebook. Placed around me, Spring Snow by Mishima Yukio, a two-cup Bialetti and a pair of stainless steel espresso cups and saucers, a scattering of my art-postcard collection and my football medal.

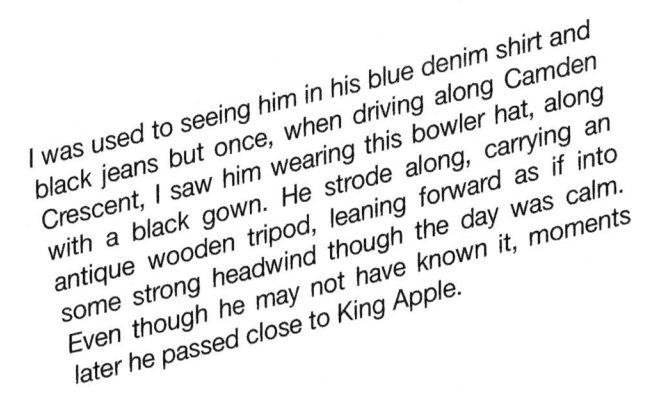

ROBINSON IN CHRONOSTASIS

I was used to seeing him in his blue denim shirt and black jeans but once, when driving along Camden Crescent, I saw him wearing this bowler hat, along with a black gown. He strode along, carrying an antique wooden tripod, leaning forward as if into some strong headwind though the day was calm. Even though he may not have known it, moments later he passed close to King Apple.

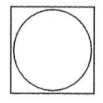

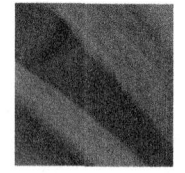

///

I take pretty much the same essential items when I go away to write; the usual digital and analogue tools of a 21st century writer, plus a threadbare Delhi-style gold/brown herringbone sleeveless jacket and just one book to read. Last time it was French Decadent Tales translated by Stephen Romer, borrowed from Libraries West.

On one rare occasion, as I walked through the university library, I saw him working on his art. My mind tried to slow down time as my eyes scanned his open notebook and the monochrome contact sheets next to it. The words and images were too small for me to make out clearly but it seemed that the past was in play. Noticing his open backpack at his feet, I formed a notion of him kitted out for occidental time travel in the 20th century; always able to pull something out of the bag to help him fit in.

<

ROBINSON IN CHRONOSTASIS

ROBINSON IN CHRONOSTASIS

We went to a pub once, and over a pint of cider, Britishness came up in conversation and as usual I steered away from it. When I returned home I studied my bookcases, questioning if my shelves of fiction and non-fiction dedicated to Morocco and Japan exemplified my Britishness.

///////////

ROBINSON IN CHRONOSTASIS

He never mentioned that he'd built a small reference collection of Britishness; it didn't occur to me to ask.

When I flew the nest aged 22, I left my local dialect behind and let Liverpool, Sheffield and Manchester shape my mouth and my words. Koji's English was very good though I think people attributed a Japanese-ness to his soft voice and polite tone.

ROBINSON IN CHRONOSTASIS

One day, when we were in conversation, he expressed an interest in a word I'd used, 'flapper'. As I explained its meaning, he took a small console from his bag and started typing. I imagined he stored words and phrases in this machine that might be useful back in time.

ROBINSON IN CHRONOSTASIS

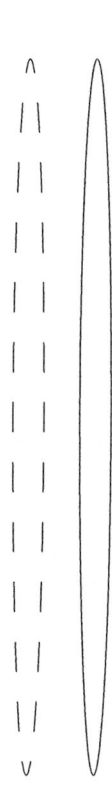

On a writing retreat in Sapporo, my non-existent command of Japanese left me feeling tired and isolated. In my room, I would console myself by looking out into the autumnal woods behind Tenjinyama Artists Retreat Centre until night came. Then I would close the curtains, lie on my bed, turn on the reading light and pick up my copy of Dance Dance Dance by Haruki Murakami which I had bought downtown in Kinokuniya Bookstore.

ROBINSON IN CHRONOSTASIS

///////

/////

ROBINSON IN CHRONOSTASIS

I imagined that no matter his travels, at the end of the day, he finds a bed, a light, a book to read, maybe the first volume of Dance to the Music of Time by Anthony Powell.

I generally travel light, I don't collect. From childhood, my stamp albums are almost empty, my Panini football sticker books incomplete. But one day, whilst trying to sort my life out, I gathered together the art postcards I'd bought as mementos of original pieces of art I'd seen and liked. I ordered a specialist postcard archive box to store them. 'Botticelli's Portrait of a Young Man' from the National Gallery, London, is at the front.

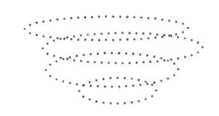

ROBINSON IN CHRONOSTASIS

When I saw his collection of photograph albums, I wondered if he knew the enormity of the histories he might be taking on.

///////

ROBINSON IN CHRONOSTASIS

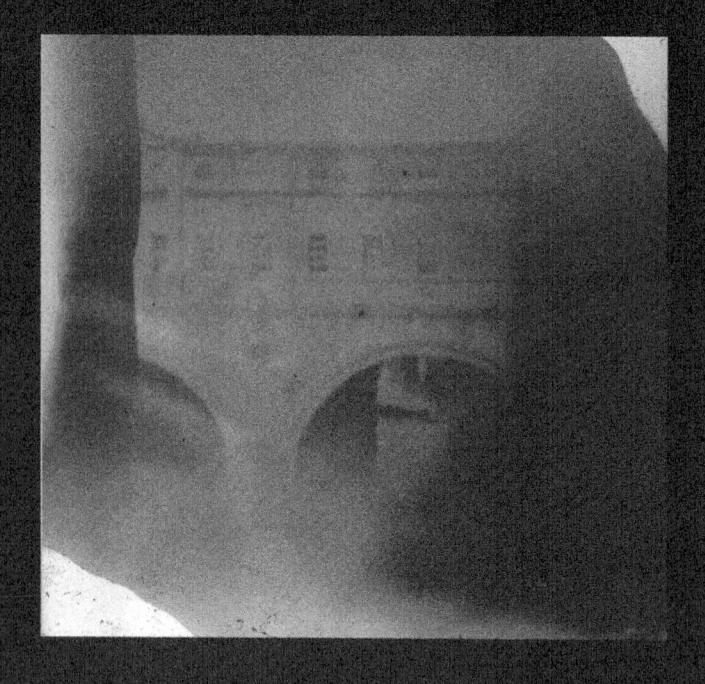

ROBINSON IN CHRONOSTASIS

I crossed Pulteney Bridge every week on my way to a meeting. It is a bridge which plays a trick; from the outside it is reminiscent of the Ponto Vecchio in Florence; but when you are on it, it looks like a normal street and the river has disappeared.

ROBINSON IN CHRONOSTASIS

ROBINSON IN CHRONOSTASIS

I'm sure that whenever he crossed that bridge, he would stop to look in the shop that sells old coins and maps - potential tokens and guides to places and times he might visit. I remember him explaining how he blended new technology with old. I wondered if it was his way to photograph the past of a place.

ROBINSON IN CHRONOSTASIS

Even though I have lived in Bath for over a decade, I sometimes feel disoriented, especially when at one of the various flea markets. I have a memory of buying two handfuls of crystal drops to use as Christmas Tree decorations. They had once been part of a chandelier in one of Bath's fine Georgian houses.

ROBINSON IN CHRONOSTASIS

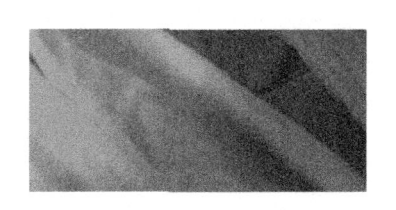

I'd heard that he had started testing his 3D time camera around the city, trying to land in the 1920s. He later told me that he'd spent many hours wandering Bath's flea markets and that one day he drifted into a reverie and over exposed the fim, burning the fringes of the memory.

////////////////

Hungry, I went downstairs to find some food. The contents of my fridge were predictable, regenerated weekly with the aid of a shopping list. Still, I eased the door open and looked inside; sheep's yoghurt, a crock of home-made Bolognese sauce, a bowl of lemons and a built-in vegetable box containing tomatoes, mushrooms, celery, ginger, carrots, green beans and a red pepper. I closed the door and turned to the bread bin, I fancied toast.

ROBINSON IN CHRONOSTASIS

ROBINSON IN CHRONOSTASIS

I guess he shares a fridge and cooks for himself, at least at the weekend. I'm not sure what I'd cook for him if he ever came round; maybe a beef stew with dumplings. We'd certainly drink the strong cider from King Apple with its complex layers of taste reflecting the summers that have passed since he first fruited in 1949.

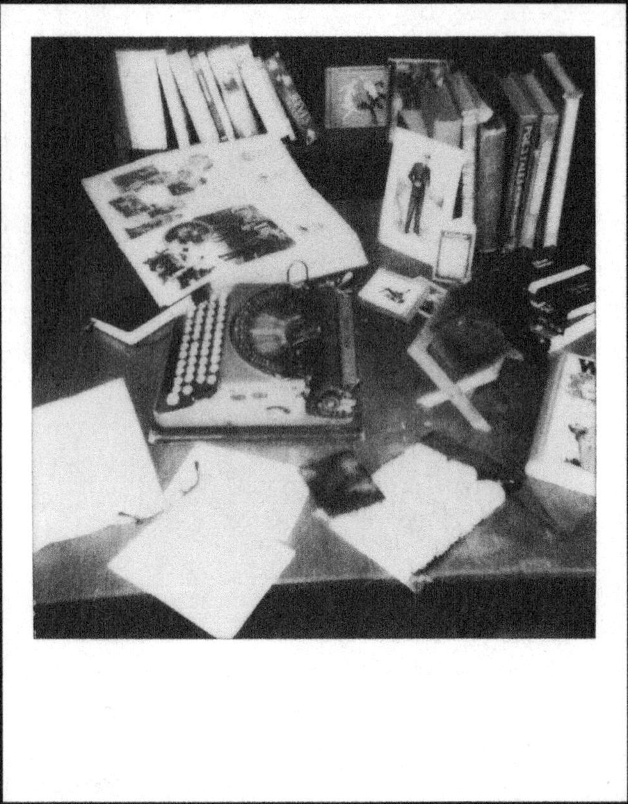

After lunch I climbed up into my loft and found the family vinyl collection going back to 1959 and all my personally recorded music cassettes since 1973. I brought them down and placed them in a cupboard with my old photograph albums and a folder containing the details of my family tree going back to the eighteenth century.

When he alluded to his time travels, I got the impression sometimes that he was trying to track down particular people in an attempt to tie up loose ends. He mentioned Paris once, another time that he'd learnt to dance The Charleston. I joked that I could imagine him dancing alongside Josephine Baker at Folies Bergère in 1925.

///////////////

ROBINSON IN CHRONOSTASIS

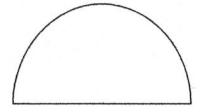

ROBINSON IN CHRONOSTASIS

////////////////

I have two boxes containing the letters I've received throughout my life from friends, lovers and family. I rummage around, poke in them sometimes, but I daren't put them in order. When Koji left Bath we started exchanging letters about our art and writing. I wrote on blue paper as it represented air mail; he used a seal on his cream envelopes depicting a winged cherub.

ROBINSON IN CHRONOSTASIS

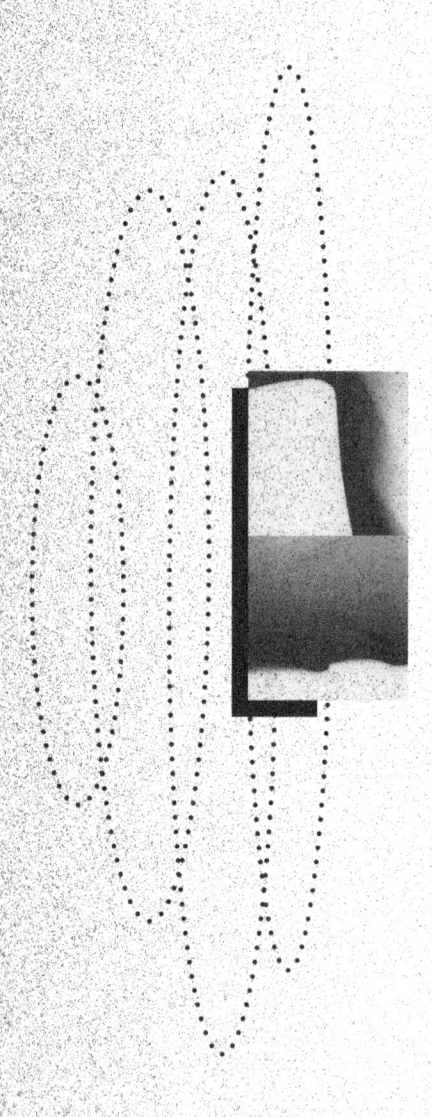

ROBINSON IN CHRONOSTASIS

He once told me that he collected old letters and I wondered if this too was about tying up loose ends. I imagined him resending the letters to their intended recipients even though he knew many would be returned by the postal services as the people or the places no longer existed. Maybe he recycled them by considering their content, and, with minimum amendments sent them to new recipients.

That night, I had dreams where I'd made simple clothes for living and practising my writing based on designs from the Modernist era.

ROBINSON IN CHRONOSTASIS

ROBINSON IN CHRONOSTASIS

I think he wore a sort of uniform; black denim trousers and blue denim shirt. Perhaps for his travels, he needed a wardrobe that could withstand the test of time and so he requisitioned batches of identical shirts that had been intended for distribution to different bodies and different lives.

Like sheep in familiar pasture we repeat our routes around this small city. I never bumped into Koji; my familiar routes, taking in the public library and pharmacy and supermarket which offered free coffee must have been different to his. However, one morning, away from my normal route, as I passed the Roman Baths I felt an urge to stop. I turned around and looked back up the Georgian street from where I'd come, sensing that someone I knew was close by.

He was amused by the fact his time travel was limited to 100 years when most of the buildings in the heart of the city were Georgian, over 200 years old.

ROBINSON IN CHRONOSTASIS

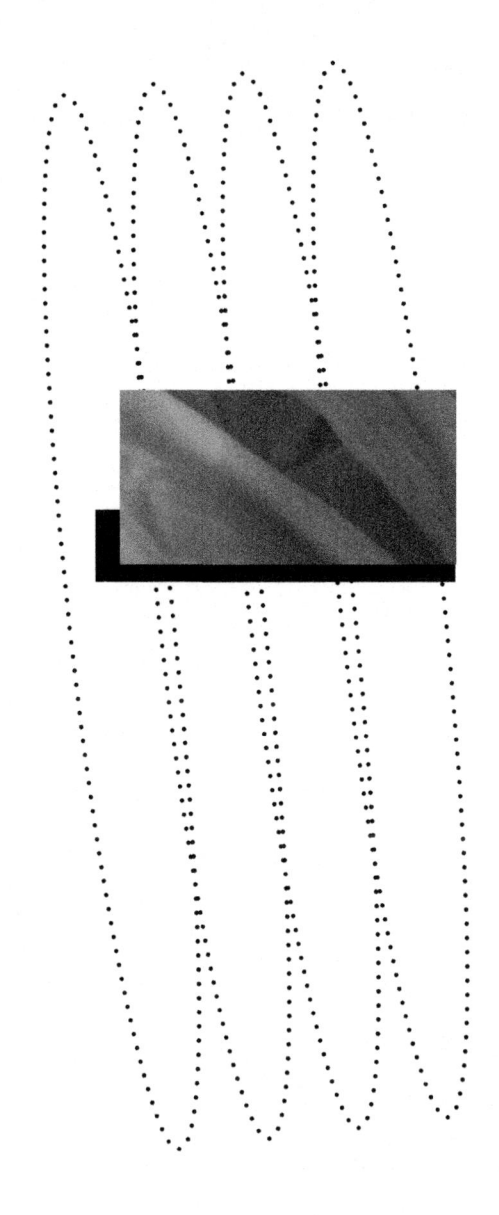

ROBINSON IN CHRONOSTASIS

One winter's day, as I crossed Upper Borough Walls, I suddenly felt vulnerable to the deep cold and arthritic damp of the place. I turned around and began to walk back up the street; my eyes began to sting and the lenses of my glasses misted. For a moment, the city seemed translucent and I could see fields, tracks and ancient orchards that I knew were no longer there.

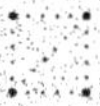

ROBINSON IN CHRONOSTASIS

Weeks later, he told me about a photograph he had taken one freezing morning and that when he developed the photograph, the pavement in the middle foreground appeared to have splintered like timber and steamlike vapours had escaped from the earth. He said that he would hit these problems some days, where time wobbles, but that he recorded these events, like the rings of King Apple.

Printed in Great Britain
by Amazon